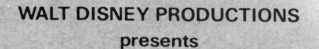

WALT DISNEY PRODUCTIONS

presents

THE
HAUNTED HOUSE

RANDOM HOUSE  NEW YORK

Library of Congress Cataloging in Publication Data
Walt Disney Productions presents The haunted house. (Disney's wonderful world of reading, #33) Out of gas, Mickey, Donald, and Pluto seek help at a spooky old house which appears to be haunted. [1. Ghost stories] I. Disney (Walt) Productions.   II. Title: The haunted house.
PZ7.W168973   [E]   75-16430   ISBN 0-394-82570-5   ISBN 0-394-92570-X (lib. bdg.).

Manufactured in the United States of America

One night Mickey and Donald were driving
down a dark road in the woods.

Pluto was riding in the back of the car.

Bats flew overhead, owls hooted,
and the wind blew through the trees.

Suddenly the old car began to sputter.
Then it rolled to a stop.
"What a place to get stuck!" said Donald.

Mickey checked the gas tank.
"We're out of gas," he said.

They walked down the road, looking for help.
After a while they saw a roof above the trees.
"Let's walk over to that house and ask for
some gas," said Donald.

Just as they reached the end of the path
the moon came out from behind a cloud.
There stood the spookiest old house
Mickey and Donald had ever seen.

"That place looks haunted," said Donald.
"I think I'll just wait here with Pluto."
"I don't believe in haunted houses,"
Mickey said. "Come with me."

Mickey and Donald crept up to the house
and peeked into a window.

"I see a light," whispered Mickey.
"Someone must be home."

Pluto was busy sniffing around.
He peeked into another window.

In the dark he saw three shadows—a fat one,
a short one, and a tall, skinny one.
Pluto began to bark and
the shadows disappeared.

Donald came over
to see why Pluto
was barking.
He looked
in the window,
but he could not
see anything.

Donald and Pluto went to the door.
Finally Mickey rang the bell.
All by itself, the door slowly opened!

They tiptoed inside.
"Is anyone home?"
called Mickey.
No one answered.

Then . . . *bang!*
The door slammed shut.
Pluto jumped into Mickey's arms.

"It's okay, boy,"
said Mickey.
"That was just the wind."

A large painting was
hanging in the hall.
"Look at that man,"
cried Donald.
"I think he's
watching us."

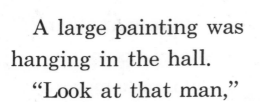

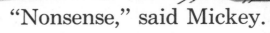

"Nonsense," said Mickey.
He walked closer
to the painting and
poked at the frame.

Zoooooooom! The wall
spun around and Mickey
disappeared.

"Where's Mickey?" Donald cried.
He and Pluto rushed to
the painting.

Donald touched the frame.

Zooooooom!
The wall spun
around again,
and Donald
and Pluto
disappeared.

They were in a dark secret passage.
There they found Mickey, too scared to speak.
For coming toward them were three ghosts—
a fat one, a short one, and a tall, skinny one.
"Go-o-o-o away! Go-o-o-o away!
Go-o-o-o-o away!" the ghosts moaned.

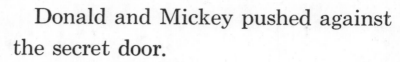

Donald and Mickey pushed against
the secret door.
But it would not open.
The ghosts kept gliding closer.

They were trapped.

Then Pluto saw a small door in the floor.

He began to bark.

"Pluto has found a way out," said Mickey.

He and Donald quickly opened the door.

All three jumped
through the opening.

Suddenly they were falling.
Down . . .

      down . . .

           down . . .
"Ow-ow-ow-ow-ow!" howled Pluto.

When they finally reached the bottom,
they landed in a large laundry basket.

Mickey, Donald, and Pluto peeked out.
Creepy spiders were crawling everywhere.

"Now do you believe in haunted houses?"
asked Donald. "We'll never get out of here."

Once more, Pluto came to their rescue.
He found an old stairway.

Mickey and Donald followed him
up the stairs.
At the top there was a heavy door.

Mickey and Donald opened the door
into a dusty old library.

Suddenly three gigantic bats swooped
down from the balcony.

Swoosh! Swoosh! They flew all around.

Pluto grabbed one of the bats and
shook it back and forth.

Sawdust flew around him.

"Now I *know* this house isn't haunted,"
cried Mickey. "These bats are fakes.
They're stuffed with sawdust."

Pluto saw a ghost
on the balcony.
He barked and barked.

"I think someone is trying
to scare us away," said Mickey.

"Well, I'm scared,"
said Donald. "Let's go!"

But before they could go anywhere,
a giant skeleton danced into the room.
He jiggled his legs.
He jiggled his arms.
"Get out of this house!" he cried.

Pluto hid behind Mickey and Donald.
They backed away from the skeleton
and bumped into a metal door.

The door flew open and they stumbled over a large pile of bags.

"These are money bags from the bank!" cried Mickey.

The skeleton came in glaring at them.
He had taken off his skeleton mask.

"I knew this house was not really haunted,"
Mickey said. "You're the one who's been
playing tricks to scare us away from here.
I bet you are a bank robber!"

"That is right," said the fat crook.

He called his two friends and they came in.
They were still wearing their ghost costumes.
"What are you going to do?" asked Mickey.

"We're going to dump you in the river,"
said the leader.
"Then we'll look for a new hideout."

The fat bank robber
grabbed Mickey.

The short one grabbed Donald.

The tall, skinny one tried to grab Pluto.

But Pluto was too fast for him.
He ran under his legs,
grabbed a money bag,
and raced out of the house.

The leader called to his skinny partner.
"Forget about that dumb dog," he said.
"Help me tie up these two troublemakers."
The robbers tied Mickey and Donald
together with a long rope.

As soon as they were alone again,
Mickey and Donald shouted for help.
But who could possibly hear them?

The robbers were busy packing up
their stolen money.

At last Mickey and Donald stopped shouting.
They knew it was hopeless.

"I wonder what happened to Pluto,"
said Donald.

"I hope he got away," said Mickey.

After a long time
the gang came back
to get Mickey
and Donald.

Just as they
reached the door,
they heard
the sound of barking.

Pluto raced into the room.
The sheriff and his men
were close behind.

Pluto ran to Mickey and Donald.
"Pluto!" cried Donald.
"You came to our rescue!"

Pluto was very glad that Mickey
and Donald were safe.
He kissed them over and over again.

The bank robbers tried to run away.
But the sheriff's men were too fast for them.

They caught the robbers and led them
to their car in handcuffs.

After Mickey and Donald had been untied,
the sheriff scratched Pluto's head.

"You sure have a smart dog," he said.
"When he brought me a money bag, I knew
he had found the bank robbers. I've been
looking all over for that gang."

By the time the sun came up, the old house
did not look haunted any more.

The sheriff held up the money bag that
Pluto had brought to him.

"The bank has asked me to give you this
as a reward for catching the robbers," he said.

"Golly," said Mickey. "Thank you."

The sheriff also gave them some gas
so that they could drive home.

On the way, they bought a bone for Pluto.

He was the one who had caught the robbers
and he deserved a reward.